CU00842154

Stories and rhymes in this book

Published by Ladybird Books Ltd
27 Wrights Lane London W8 5TZ
A Penguin Company
3 5 7 9 10 8 6 4 2

© LADYBIRD BOOKS LTD MCMXCVIII

Produced for Ladybird Books Ltd by Nicola Baxter and Amanda Hawkes

The moral rights of the author/illustrator have been asserted
LADYBIRD and the device of a Ladybird are trademarks of Ladybird Books Ltd
All rights reserved. No part of this publication may be reproduced,
stored in a retrieval system, or transmitted in any form or by any
means, electronic, mechanical, photocopying, recording or otherwise,
without the prior consent of the copyright owner.

Printed in Italy

The Bouncy Bunnies

by Irene Yates

illustrated by Jill Newton

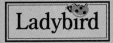

BOUNCING... BOING!

See the Bouncy Bunnies...
Bounce!

Bounce!

Bounce!

Bouncing high,

Bouncing low,

Bouncing everywhere they go!

BOUNCY BUNNY BURROW

Over the hills...

and across the fields...

and down in the valley, lies Bouncy Bunny Burrow.

The Bouncy Bunnies who live there NEVER keep still, so nobody knows EXACTLY how many there are.

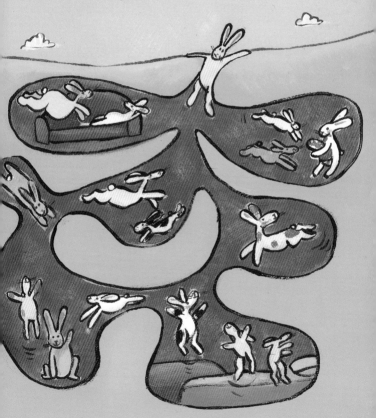

But there are a LOT!

"How CAN I remember all their birthdays?" said Great Grandfather Bouncy Bunny one day.

He tried to write them down in a l-o-n-g list.

But when he had written just half the bunnies' names, the list was TOO long...

and another ten baby bunnies had been born!

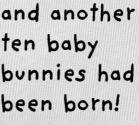

"I know!" he said at last. "Let's pretend ALL the bunnies have the SAME birthday.

We can have one BIG, HUGE, ENORMOUS birthday party every year!"

And everyone cheered
because that was a
BRILLIANT idea!

DO THE BOUNCE!

Put your paws
in the air,
Then bend
your knees.

Twitch your
nose as if
you're going
to sneeze.

Fall on your front paws,
Wiggle your rump,

Then...
Feet close
together,
Get ready
to...

MR FARMER'S NUMBER

Mr Farmer grows carrots and cabbages for the Bouncy Bunnies.

One day he decided to count the bunnies, so that he could plant enough vegetables.

He stood at the side of the field with his clipboard and pencil.

"Over here all bunnies, please! Come and stand in line!"

Out came all the Bouncy Bunnies from their burrows.

But could they stand still in a line? They could NOT!

BOUNCE! they went.

THE BOUNCING SONG

The Bouncy Bunnies
All day long,
While they're bouncing,
Sing this song:

Bounce in
the morning,

Bounce at
night,

Bounce into view,

And bounce out of sight.

Bounce with a somersault,

Bounce with
a flounce,

Bounce with
a backwards
flip,

Bounce with
a BOUNCE!

BABIES WHO BOUNCE

Bouncy Bunny babies can't bounce very well to start with...

so their mothers take them along to a Fussy Old Aunt Bouncy Bunny to learn.

The Fussy Old Aunt Bouncy Bunny plops all the babies on to the bouncing mat.

They lie on their backs...

and kick their paws in the air...

and cry for their bunny mummies.

"That's enough!" calls the Fussy Old Aunt. Then she blows her whistle.

The Bouncy Bunny babies stop crying and roll over on to their tummies.

They push themselves up on to their back legs and all hold paws.

The Fussy Old Aunt plays bouncing tunes on the old Bouncy Bunny piano.

The Bouncy Bunny babies jig up and down to the music...

faster...   and faster...

and before they know what they are doing, they're BOUNCING!

And all the bunnies gurgle and giggle because they're SO happy.

CAREFUL BOUNCING

Even if they're
in a hurry,
Bunnies NEVER
bounce or scurry,
When there is
a road to cross.

The Crossing Bunny
is the boss!

THE BOUNCING RACE

One day nine of the Bouncy Bunnies decided to have a bouncing race.

They all began to line up for the start. There were...

Bouncer, Flouncer, Pouncer,

Jumper, Bumper, Thumper,

Leaper, Peeper and Sleeper.

At the last minute, along came Hopper.

The other Bouncy Bunnies laughed at him. "You'll never win! We're all much better bouncers than you!"

Poor Hopper.
He wasn't
very good at
bouncing.

However
hard he
tried, he
always
ended up
bouncing on
one foot.

But a Granny
Bouncy Bunny
whispered...

"Pretend your
back feet
are stuck
together
with gum!"

Then she said,
"Ready! Steady! Go!"

"Gum, gum, gum!" said Hopper to himself all the way down the track.

He kept his back feet together and didn't hop at all.

And every bunny cheered
because, even though he
didn't win, he BOUNCED
all the way!

FIVE BOUNCY BUNNIES

Five Bouncy Bunnies,
In the carrot store,

One had a tummy ache,
And then there were four!

Four Bouncy
Bunnies,
Sitting
underneath
a tree,

Down fell an apple,
And then there were three!

Three Bouncy Bunnies,
Playing Tag and Boo,

One hid in the cabbages,
And then there were two.

Two Bouncy Bunnies,
Having lots of fun,
One bounced off
To see his gran...

And then there
was one.

One Bouncy Bunny,
Bouncing in the sun,

Down came the rain,
And then there were none!